Assiyah in The City

A Journey about Empathy

Green Fig

By: Zeina El-Chaar

Illustrated By:

CHY Illustration & Design

Name

_____

Publisher: Green Fig
Pennsylvania, USA
www.gogreenfig.com
info@gogreenfig.com

Green Fig

Pure Hearts
Strong Minds

Dear Parents And Educators,

We are pleased to welcome you and your children back to the series **"Pure Hearts, Strong Minds"** with a new book **"Assiyah in the City"**. This story aims to help children develop empathy and compassion, guided by the Hadith of the Prophet, may peace be upon him: "One of you will not have complete faith until one loves for others what one loves for oneself." While reading **Assiyah in the City** with your child, please take the opportunity to deepen your connection, encourage reflection, and share examples from your daily life. Do not hesitate to lead by example and be a model for them through your actions and words as they imitate more of what you do than what you say.

Empathy in children is a quality built over time and strengthened through their surroundings' influence and teaching. Empathy is the ability to understand others' emotions, be sensitive to them, and to put oneself in other people's shoes. Through empathy, a child understands the positive and negative effects of their actions on others. How does empathy develop?
First, it develops by receiving compassion, love, and kindness from you. This produces a strong sense of secure attachment, which serves as a foundation for your child to offer compassion and kindness in return. Second, as your child begins to understand their own needs, emotions, and ways of communicating with others, they learn to regulate their emotions and responses with the guidance of adults. As emotional intelligence develops, the child gains social skills, learns to share, be assertive, offers help, approaches others, and more. The early years of a child's life are a precious time to help them learn to put themselves in other people's shoes, understand their needs, and, subsequently, develop a sense of mutual aid, empathy, and even love for others what they love for themselves.

Zeina El-Chaar M.sc. Ps.ed

Strategies and ideas for parents and educators to develop empathy in children:

- Tell stories of positive role models and people from our history and rich heritage. Talk to children about their good behaviors.

- Ask the child questions: "How would you feel in this situation?" or "What do you think the other person is feeling?"

- Offer opportunities for the child to show empathy without forcing it too much. Let the child realize good actions at their own pace and encourage their autonomy to do so. For example, "Would you like to give your old toys to children in need?"

- Explain to the child the benefits of their actions without over praising them. For example, "People feel so relieved when they receive help whenever they are in need."

- Use different occasions to show generosity without expecting a return. Your child watches you and will want to imitate you. For example, 'Eid, Ramadan, and back to school.

- Be generous to your child and show them that you appreciate them as a person. Speak well of them to other family members. In general, children who know they are loved and appreciated will love and appreciate others.

- Wait until the child is calm and receptive (so they have managed their own emotions) before talking to them about other people's emotions and the effect of their behavior. The younger the child, the more difficult for him or her to be able to put themselves in other people's shoes.

- Explain to them from an early age the notion of sincerity in actions, seeking only God's acceptance.

- As a family, volunteer or contribute to many charitable projects.

- Play collaborative games with your child.

Mistakes to avoid:

- Making the child feel guilty or comparing them to others if they do not show empathy, which can make them feel inferior. For example, "You are the only one who doesn't do it" or "You see, your cousin lends his toys". Teach them or show them ways to do it instead.

- Forcing the child to interact with others too quickly. Respect your child's pace; children are all different. Do it gradually and encourage them by implementing small steps so that they experience success. For example, do not force a child who is very shy to offer food for guests.

- Overpraising the child or overvaluing their actions after a good deed. Be careful not to exaggerate; be discreet. A simple thank you or mentioning that we are proud of them is enough.

- Speaking ill of people in front of your child or attributing bad intentions to them. For example, "If he acted like that with us, he certainly does not love us or is jealous of us."

Phrases you can use to support this process in children:

• I am proud to be your parent.

• You are a good child. May God protect you.

• Your actions are very beneficial and have surely brought comfort.

• I admire your courage and empathy.

• How can I help you achieve what you want to do? (Support the idea or project of the child).

• We can only do our best to offer help. God is the Creator of sustenance and help.

• Just as we have many blessings, we share and give some of them to help others.

• I am praying for you to be among the well guided, God willing.

• I believe in you and your dreams (I trust in your adilities and good aspirations).

• I am here for you; you can count on me.

"Come on, wake up beautiful Assiyah!" Assiyah's father opens the curtains wide to wake her up, today is the big day! Assiyah is going with her dad to work. They have to go to the big construction site in the city center where her father is helping build a large hospital.

"Yes, Dad! I'm waking up." says Assiyah, her eyes still closed with fatigue as she stretches and yawns, putting her hand over her mouth.

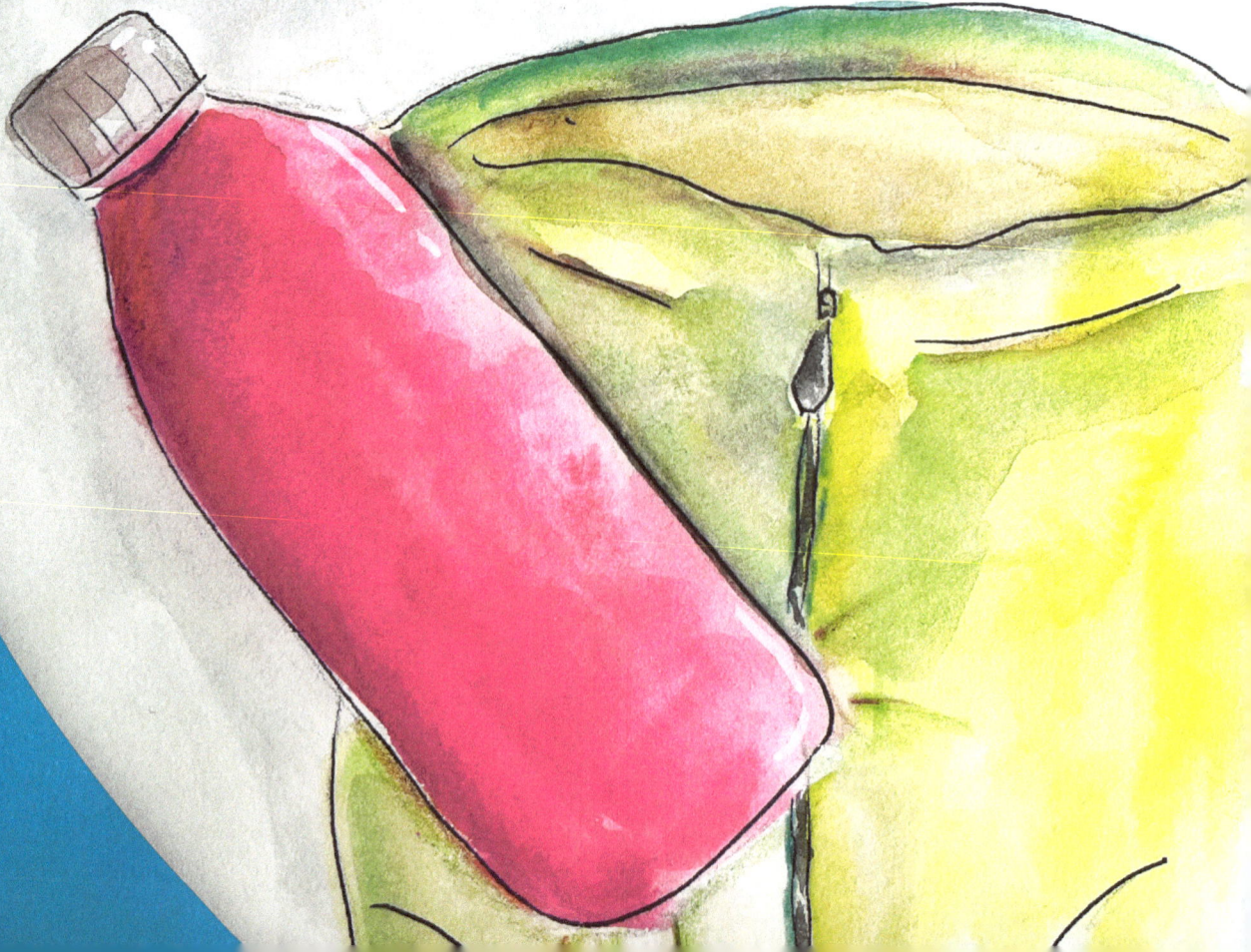

"Are you still sure you want to come with me? It will be a long day, I have to check on the progress and we will be spending the day in the city center," says her father.

"Yes, Dad, I'm sure. I can't wait to see the big buildings and take the subway with you," Assiyah replies.

"Very well. Let's go then. Don't forget your snacks, water, and jacket in case it gets cold." Assiyah is used to preparing her things herself, and she knows what she needs when she gets hungry, cold, or tired. So, as soon as everything is ready, she and her father head to the bus for a long and beautiful day.

Assiyah is curious about what she will discover. She gazes out the window with big eyes as the driver lets different passengers in to drop them off at the subway station.

Looking out the window, she sees an elderly women waiting for cars to stop in order to cross the street. She looks at her attentively and thinks that this women must need help.
The driver continues on his way and arrives at the subway stop. Assiyah and her father thank the driver, get off the bus, and head towards the subway.

Assiyah is impressed. How big and busy it is! There are people everywhere. She holds her father's hand even tighter, feeling a certain fear in her heart.

As she turns her head, Assiyah sees a mother with a big pregnant belly sighing while holding her back and pushing a stroller with a young child in it with the other hand. She looks at her attentively and thinks that this mother looks tired and needs to rest. She gives her a timid little smile before turning her head. As she and fer father embark on the subway, she also observes the young man who gives his seat to her on the subway.

After about 20 minutes, a voice announces that the passengers have now arrived to the city center.

"Did we arrive? Am I finally going to see the hospital construction site?" Assiyah asks.

"Yes, my dear. Stay close to me and let's go," says her father.

Leaving the subway and heading towards the city's main avenues, Assiyah sees a man sitting on the ground. He has several bags around him, looks sad and tired, and his hands and face are quite dirty. Assiyah looks at him attentively.

"Dad, what's wrong with this man? Why is he sitting on the ground like that?" she asks hesitantly.

"My dear, he is a homeless person. A homeless person is someone who does not have a home. They live on the street and search for food every day," says her father. Assiyah feels her heart tighten a little. She looks at him attentively and thinks that he needs to eat and take a shower.

She gives him a timid little smile as her father gives him a few dollars and they continue on their way.

Arriving at the construction site, Assiyah is dazzled by the big building that will soon become the hospital her father is helping to build. She looks at all the lights and the many cars waiting in traffic. She sees the skyscrapers and the buildings. She hears cars honk and people talking loudly. Her father shows her the work being done and invites her to rest in a beautiful, well-ventilated office.

Assiyah feels a little relief as it is very hot and dusty outside. Through the window, she sees a worker talking on the phone and crying. Her father explains that he is a migrant worker who traveled here for work and has not seen his children in five months. She looks at him closely and thinks that this person must be sad and needs comfort. Assiyah feels a little pinch in her heart.

A long day passed and Assiyah's dad finished work finally! Assiyah is tired and can't wait to go to the big park in the city center with her father, where he promised to stop by to get her a snack and let her play. Assiyah talks to her father about everything she saw, walking quickly and looking at all the big park trees.

Suddenly, she spots a young boy near the ice cream vendor. He seems to be her age with brown hair and a red pullover and blue pants. He is sitting in a chair with big wheels on both sides. It's a wheelchair.

The boy is sitting alone and not talking to anyone. She looks at him closely and turns to look in the same direction as him. She sees a group of children flying beautiful, colorful kites. The children run, laugh, and spin around happily.

She then turns to the boy who is sitting there, not saying a word. She feels her heart tighten again.

At this moment, her father calls her from afar to go back home. "It's been a long day, Assiyah. Let's go home now," he says. Assiyah follows her father, thanks him for the day, and continues on her way. However, something in her has changed. She doesn't want to laugh and talk like she did in the morning.

Assiyah can't stop thinking about this boy. She doesn't know if he was sad, bored, or just calm. She begins to wonder if he would have liked to play like the others.

Arriving home, Assiyah prepares to go to bed. Her heart is still a little tight, so she decides to talk to her dad just before she sleeps.

"Dad, do you remember when I was telling you about the people I saw today? There was a boy in the park too. He watched other children playing with their kites while he stayed in his wheelchair watching. I wonder how he feels,» Assiyah says. "You know, my beautiful daughter, what you did today was putting yourself in other people's shoes," explains her father.

"What? Shoes?" Assiyah says, confused. "Yes. You thought about their needs, and what you would have wanted if you were in their place. Like when you saw the elderly women crossing the street who needed help, the mom with babies who needed rest, the homeless man who needed food, and the worker who needed comfort. You managed to put yourself in their shoes and understand them. That's what empathy is, my dear."

"You know, our Prophet, may peace be upon him, taught us to be empathetic towards others and to want for them what we want for ourselves. He said in a Hadith that one will not have complete faith until one loves for others what one loves for oneself. I'm glad to see you thinking about others like that," her father continues.

Assiyah listens carefully. She still thinks about the little boy. She thinks about what he would have liked and wanted. She thinks about him until she drifts off to sleep.

The next morning, at sunrise, Assiyah wakes up wide eyed. She still feels her heart tighten, but knows that it is because she thinks that the boy must be sad and wants to have fun too.

She rushes to her father who is already in the kitchen drinking his coffee.

"Dad, dad! I have an idea. Please let me come with you to work today too. But I want to stop by the toy store first." Her father gives her a wink, meaning, "of course."

MENU

After a long day, Assiyah finally arrives at the park. She's carrying a big bag and has a big smile on her face.

To her surprise, she realizes that the boy is not there. She looks everywhere, walks around the park, and there is no sign of him.

Her father suggests that they ask the ice cream man. He takes her hand and goes to talk to him.

"The boy you're looking for is Dylan, he is my nephew. He comes to keep me company sometimes. Dylan is an orphan, and my wife and I take care of him. He stayed home today."

Assiyah then has a disappointed look. She would have liked to show him the surprise.

"He will be here tomorrow though," says the ice cream seller.

"Okay, thank you sir. Have a nice day." Assiyah then leaves with her father, hand in hand.

As if on a mission, Assiyah makes the same journey the next day. She goes downtown again, takes the bus, gets on the subway, goes to the construction site, and waits in the room where her father works.

After a long day, Assiyah found Dylan in the park, in the same place. He still had the same sad look on his face. He is sitting next to his uncle, watching the passersby and animals in the park.

With great courage, Assiyah approaches him and introduces herself: "My name is Assiyah. What's your name?"

"My name is Dylan," he says with a surprised look.
"Your uncle told us that you would be here today. I know you don't know me, but I want to give you something. I know that I would have wanted it, so I want to give it to you," Assiyah says.

The young boy looks a little shy. He opens the bag while his eyes widen, and a smile appears on his face. He sees a big colorful kite, even bigger than all the ones he saw before.

With a big smile, he looks at Assiyah and her father and thanks them warmly. He quickly unpacks the toy and examines it, saying "wow" and "ooh".

Assiyah's heart doesn't feel tight anymore. In that moment, she feels a joy similar to the boy's. She is happy to have done this beautiful gesture for him and feels just as happy as the boy is right now. She is also pleased to apply the teachings of her beloved Prophet and help others.

For the rest of the afternoon, the two children have so much fun at the park. Assiyah pushes the boy in the wheelchair as he tries to make the kite fly as high as possible.

What a beautiful afternoon that neither will forget!

The End

Strategies for children:

Questions to ask myself before saying or doing something:

- If it were me, what would I have wanted?

- How could this person feel?

- What might this person need?

- How can I help?

- Does this person really want my help or does he or she prefer space?

- What good deed can I do for my family?

- What good deed can I do for my community and friends?

- Am I doing this (action) for the right reason, because I am sincere?

How can I help, be empathetic and apply the Hadith of my Prophet:

- Giving away my old toys with good intentions (with my parents' permission). I can even give a new one to a child who appreciates it.

- Helping an elderly person cross the street.

- Helping my parents prepare the meal.

- Removing from the street anything that might hinder or hurt others.

- Helping my brother or sister with their homework or tasks.

- If I have water, I can offer a drink to someone who needs it as much as I do, first.

- Baking a cake and giving it to my neighbors.

- Let other friends play first and wait my turn.

- To console a friend who is sad. Listen to them and ask them if I can help.

www.ingramcontent.com/pod-product-compliance
Lightning Source LLC
LaVergne TN
LVHW072130070426
835513LV00002B/43